The Wineglass

A PASSOVER STORY

By Norman Rosten 1914-

ILLUSTRATIONS BY KAETHE ZEMACH

First published in the United States of America in 1978
by the Walker Publishing Company, Inc.

Published simultaneously in Canada
by Beaverbooks, Limited, Pickering, Ontario.

Trade ISBN: 0-8027-6318-9
Reinf. ISBN: 0-8027-6319-7

Library of Congress Catalog Card Number: 77-16758

Previously published as a chapter
in *Under the Boardwalk* by Norman Rosten.

Printed in the United States of America
10 9 8 7 6 5 4 3 2 1

If the Sun and Moon should doubt,
They'd immediately go out.

William Blake

I T WAS the time of the Holidays, the weather bringing a hint of summer. The grownups took it very seriously. I had to do the same. You can't laugh at something when everyone else around you believes in it. Everybody acted strangely during this period, they cried a little then laughed so hard you didn't know what to believe. But the whole thing, the Holiday itself, Passover, was serious I guess. After all, you couldn't celebrate all that religion and history just for fun. The children of ancient Israel being chased out of Egypt by the Pharaoh after suffering all kinds of plagues, and then Moses leading them into the wilderness—if that isn't serious I don't know what is.

And there was my grandfather. I wanted to be serious just for him. On the Holidays I always tried to behave as best I could, to make him happy. He was a little scary, my grandfather, with his large face and heavy beard and his eyes looking right into you. But I knew he was kind. He liked me even though I had disappointed him by not going to religious school. I went for a while, but the long hours at a desk with a language I could never grasp soon made me ill. I complained of headaches. My mother said I was working too hard. But it was my father who decided that I go to public school only. I felt better.

Often, on the Sabbath eve, I watched my grandfather give the blessings over food. He recited them with his eyes closed, like he had a secret he didn't want to share. On the Holidays, the prayers got worse, they didn't stop for days, a whole week, they were all about suffering and miracles. God and the prophets were running around all the time in those early times. You didn't know what to believe.

I discussed the whole thing with my friend Jimmy Berkowitz. "Aah, it's all fairy tales, all that stuff," commented Jimmy with derision. "Like Moses lifting his arm and telling the Red Sea to move back so they could cross over on dry land. You believe that?"

"Well, it could happen," I said.

"The sea could divide in *half*, you believe it?"

"If it was a miracle," I insisted. "Things like that are miracles, so you gotta believe." I never knew how to answer him.

He leered at me. "C'mon, we'll go to the ocean right now and

I'll lift my arm and holler 'Go back, water, I wanna cross over to New Jersey.' What do you think would happen? Right— nuthin'."

"Yeah, but if it was like a great emergency, and you were a leader—" I persisted.

"That's for the birds!" he cut in. "You go to the synagogue on the Holy Days?"

"Sometimes."

"Don't your parents go?"

"Only my grandparents. My mother, sometimes. My father, never. He says it's all a fake, God is a fake."

Jimmy whistled in admiration. "Boy, I hate to think what'll happen to your old man if God is really up there waiting for him. Poom! One look and he's the Invisible Man!" He laughed and slapped his head and hopped on one leg pretending to shake water out of his ear.

I was alarmed at the thought of God punishing my father or making him invisible. "God would never do that. He forgives you if you mean well."

Jimmy was relentless. "Your old man is gonna fry like a hot dog at Nathan's, ho, ho!" And he ran off, leaving me with a hollow twinge near my heart. I felt a thrill of identification with my father. Imagine, to call God a fake, that was bravery! My father was brave, no matter what anyone could say about him. I saw my father facing God, and God would say: I exist and you have made a terrible mistake and you will pay the penalty, and my father would look right back at Him and say: I am ready, and God would say: Who else didn't believe in me? Did your son believe? (I shivered, waiting his reply.) And he said: Yes, he believes.

My father lied to save me! But if it was a lie, God would know (God Almighty, All-Seeing, All-Knowing), and He might strike me down. Maybe on the Passover Holiday He was testing me, to see what I would do. I bet He didn't like me listening to Jimmy. I got a cold sweat thinking about it.

My uncles didn't believe in God, I could tell, but my aunts did, and my grandfather most of all. Sometimes I got the idea he thought *he* was God, I mean the way he acted, very slow and important and wise, the way he lifted his arm when he asked for a glass of water (Moses lifting his arm to the Red Sea!) or how he smoothed his beard so carefully. Well, if he didn't think he was God, I bet he thought he was pretty close. He prayed

like he was real close, like God was watching him personally, breathing down his neck almost.

Passover night arrived. The relatives filled up all the places around the table, joking and teasing, while Grandfather looked over the assemblage like a big rough-combed rooster counting his family. The Holiday had lots of funny dishes and prayers. There was one big dish with bitter herbs and vegetables, float-

ing in salt water, also a combination of nuts, apples, raisins, a
roasted lamb bone, and a roasted egg. Also, four cups of wine
were to be drunk by every member of the family seated around
the table. Not to mention having to listen to the stories and
songs all about being chased out of Egypt, mixed with prayers.
Whenever my sister and cousins giggled or grew restless,
Grandfather's eyes (Dracula's eyes!) would fix us with a relent-

11

less gaze that froze us to attention. It was hard to listen and not understand. I liked the singsong parts, but after a while I got sleepy and had to fight to keep awake.

In front of each place on the table was a wineglass filled with wine. At certain times in the ceremony, the grownups would lift their glasses and take a swallow. But there was one glass that held my attention. It was the special glass no one lifted. That

glass, they told me, was reserved for the angel Elijah. The door to the room remained slightly ajar for Elijah to enter if he so wished, and to be refreshed by the wine. A messenger of God, who could come as a guest. An angel to visit us! What if he chose to visit us this night, to come to this house of all the houses in the world? The idea of a real angel entering the room made me giddy. Was it possible? Did they believe it, or was it a game? Could an angel come in through the small opening of the door? I guess it could squeeze through sideways, or maybe it floated through like smoke—did anyone ever *see* an angel? Suppose it lifted the glass—but that would be impossible. It probably just bent down and took a sip. How much could an angel sip? Could an angel get drunk, I wondered?

All these questions raced around in my head along with the murmuring prayers. I once wanted to ask my grandfather some of these questions, but I was afraid he'd become angry. You had to be careful of what you asked an old religious man, especially if he gave you a nickel sometimes.

Grandfather was booming along with the ceremony. I tried to follow him in the little book which had the Jewish letters running from right to left on one half of the page, and the

English translation going from left to right on the other half. I was skipping lots of words, but I knew enough to keep track of him.

" . . . our God, King of the Universe, who hast kept us alive, and hast maintained us, and hast enabled us to reach this time . . ." Then washing hands. Then dipping greens in salt water. "Blessed art thou, Lord, our God, King of the Universe, who dost create the fruit of the soil . . ." Then breaking half of the matzah and lifting the ceremonial plate. "This is the poor bread which our fathers ate in the land of Egypt. Let anyone who is hungry, come in and eat; let anyone who is needy, come in and make Passover. This year we are here; next year we shall be in the land of Israel. This year we are slaves; next year we shall be freemen."

Then he turned to me, at the same time removing the ceremonial plate and pouring a second cup. I was the youngest, and I had to do this next thing, which was called The Four Questions. I had it memorized. "Why is this night different from all other nights? On all other nights, we eat leavened bread and matzah; on this night, we eat only matzah. On all other nights, we eat all kinds of herbs; on this night, we eat mainly bitters.

On all other nights, we do not dip even once; on this night, we dip twice . . ." I was going along great. My grandfather—I could see him out of the corner of my eye—looked pleased. (Maybe he'd give me a dime before he left!)

Then it happened. I saw it happening. The angel entered the room. Elijah, thin and pale, looking at no one, glided in, floated in, and stopped. He wore clothes, but not like any clothes I could recognize, more like a silky cloak that ruffled in the breeze. But there was no breeze—we were in a room! His face turned toward me but he did not see me. It was a face of eager and luminous beauty, a light seemed to come from within it and radiated outward. All the while his clothes stirred as though by a delicate wind. He slowly moved toward the table where the solitary untouched wineglass waited. He saw the glass and bent forward, leaning down. . .

I shouted, "The angel. I see the angel!"

They stared at me, my grandfather, grandmother, father, mother, sister, uncles, aunts, and cousins. Their faces swayed before me.

"What's with you?" my grandfather spoke hoarsely.

"The angel. Right next to you!"

"Why are you interrupting?" he sputtered. "Be quiet or leave the room."

The angel seemed like a mist before my eyes. His lips were now touching the rim of the wineglass.

"Look," I whispered, and pointed.

Nobody moved. They thought I was crazy. I heard my mother's reassuring but urgent voice. "What is it? What do you see?"

"The angel," I moaned. "Drinking the wine."

My grandfather exploded. "Get the boy out of here. What angel? What are you talking about? You don't see an angel. Only God can see one!"

"I see him. I see him!" I screamed.

My mother was alarmed and came over to me, putting her arm around my shoulder. Now my father rose from his chair in a sudden movement. "The boy has a fever. And why? I will tell you why." He turned and spoke directly to my grandfather. "Because you have stuffed his head with nonsense, with foolish stories, with God and angels and miracles. Every month it's something else, another holiday, another miracle of the Jews. Enough miracles!" His face was flushed, his fingers red from gripping the table. "This is America. Nobody believes in such stories anymore."

Grandfather roared back. "I believe. That is enough!"

"Believe by yourself, then!"

"God's wrath will strike you one day. You have violated the Holy Days. You have labored on these days—"

My father slammed the table. "I will do what I please. And you be careful or you won't be allowed inside this house, do you hear me?"

My mother started to cry. Uncle Ezra reached for a radish and tipped over his wineglass. My aunts and cousins sat rigidly in their chairs. Uncle Morty flung down his napkin. "It's a bughouse here!" My grandmother shouted, "What's happening? Why don't we sing?"

All this must have scared the angel, because he got smaller and smaller and finally vanished.

"He's going away," I wailed softly.

"Be quiet," said my father grimly. "Not another word from you. Go to your room." Then, to Grandfather, "Finish this business tonight, but without me, and without the boy. And tomorrow night, please, pray somewhere else."

My mother wept openly, loudly, despairingly. My father turned to the others. "Let her cry. The father sings, the daughter

19

cries. Each has a trick." He passed me at the door where I had lingered. "Go to bed," he said in an iron voice and vanished.

My grandfather hurled a final thunderbolt at his back. "Satan!" he hissed. And then, to me, quivering, "An angel, hah! If it was given to anyone to see this angel, then it would be me. Is that clear? And another thing, my little dreamer, He would not send His angel to this house of anti-God!"

"Then why do you keep the wineglass ready?" I pleaded. They were all silent now, watching.

"Why? It's the ceremony."

"Then it's not true?"

"Of course it's true," he snapped. "A thing does not have to happen to be true. To see a thing doesn't prove anything. *Belief* is what proves."

He was confusing me again, like all the grownups. "Well, I saw it!" I shot back at him and ran out. I heard behind me the sudden buzz of talk, my aunts now getting into the act, and above the voices flying across the air behind me, the sound of my mother's weeping followed until I reached my room and shut the door. I was sad, and leaned against the window where my eye caught a cluster of stars far away over the rooftop, millions of miles away. Was God up there, really watching everybody? The stars seemed to tremble, as if they wanted to speak.

It was hours later when my grandfather stopped in to say good night. I didn't know what to say and was glad when he spoke first. "Are you all right, boy?" he asked gently.

"Yes, Grandpa."

"Such noise on a holiday I don't enjoy," he said with a careless gesture of his hand that nevertheless gave him dignity. "Your mother is suffering, and your father, excuse me, such a man I don't understand." I nodded, not wanting to get him started on my father. He coughed, turned to go, then stopped.

"What is it?" I knew he wanted to ask me something.

"Tell me . . ." He sat down heavily on the chair near the bed. He took a deep breath. "You said you saw the angel. You truly saw it?"

"Yes. I think so."

"You think so." His voice bristled.

"I did. I really did, Grandpa."

"It spoke to you?"

"No."

That seemed to satisfy him. "You imagined it."

"I don't think so."

He squirmed in his chair. "But if God would send an angel to this poor house, if He truly did, why should He give you alone the power to see it? I am closer to Him, I pray to Him every day in the year, already for over sixty years. Why should it appear to you only?"

"I don't know, Grandpa." I sighed, watching his perplexed face, the exhaustion in his eyes. I thought of his believing, year after year, when everywhere around him the world was changing. Soon he would die, my grandmother too, and what would happen? Would their ideas and beliefs die? In the streets nearby, older people, Italians mostly, sometimes spoke in another language. They would sing, too. I would often play in those streets, and the air sounded with shouts I couldn't understand. Fat ladies and skinny men and skinny and fat the other way around hobbled in and out of dark hallways jabbering away in a high rapid music. Then, on my own street, I would hear another kind of jabber mixed with words I could understand, as though one language was struggling with the other. It all sounded funny. I guess they believed in all the things they brought over with them—the candles and baking and holidays and awful funerals. But mostly joy. Even in the dark houses, facing the alleyways, even in the streets where their children's children played, growing into the ways of another land, they still clung to their own ways. What would happen when all the old people from the old countries died here? There would be a different life in the houses, I knew that. Different forever.

I knew I would miss my grandfather, and right now I didn't want to hurt him. He looked at me with deep hollow eyes. I wanted to comfort him, my heart flowed toward him. "Maybe I didn't see an angel after all," I said. "It happened so quick, and the white curtain moved, maybe it was the curtain . . ." I didn't want to believe it. I didn't want it to be true. It couldn't be true anyway. An angel was not a real thing. It was in the Bible and fairy tales, and sometimes in songs where girls were like angels, but what did that prove? No, I imagined it, because they were singing about angels, and the wineglass was there, waiting . . .

"All right," he said, rising. "We won't talk about it anymore. And don't please talk about it in the street. An angel is sacred. God does not like little boys talking about angels like they were potatoes, you understand?"

24

"Yes, Grandpa."

"So . . . good night." He reached into his pocket and withdrew a coin. "Here's ten cents for a Happy Holiday."

"Gee, thanks, Grandpa." I reached up to kiss his cheek.

"No more angels!" His voice was now imperious, but not unkind. He walked out with little shuffling steps.

I finished reading a Frank Merriwell book in less than an hour, undressed, and got into bed. I tried not to think of the angel, but all of a sudden it popped into my mind: the halo! He didn't have one! If it was Elijah, a messenger of God, shouldn't he have worn a halo? I didn't remember a halo. Then it was . . . the curtains moving. I tried hard to go to sleep so I would stop thinking, but the harder I tried the more wide-awake I remained.

I didn't hear my mother enter. The room was dark and she sat at the edge of the bed, her body shook with brief silent spasms of weeping. Should I pretend to be asleep? Her hand touched my forehead.

I spoke. "I'm all right, Momma. Don't worry."

"Terrible, terrible," she murmured. "He's so hard to live with. I married him, I must have loved him. But what he did tonight I will never forgive. Never. To shame my own father, to

make fun of what other people believe . . ." She squeezed my hand, and continued, "And not to believe you, his own son, is the worst thing of all."

"Did you believe me?" There was a hush in the room.

"Yes."

My heart tripped with joy. "You believe I saw the angel?"

"Of course."

"But why didn't anyone else see it? Why didn't Grandpa see it, the way he talks to God practically every day?"

My mother's voice was soothing in the darkness. "Because nobody else wanted to believe it like you did. You wanted to see the angel so much that he came to you. There are angels everywhere, good and bad, beautiful and ugly, and you can call them. Not everyone can. But you can. And tonight, you saw what nobody else in the world saw."

I was dazzled by this thought. It made me sleepy. My mother said, "I will always believe what you say." She kissed me and left the room. I never remembered such happiness.

I fell asleep, and awoke with a start. Was it a minute or hours later? A thought, running inside my head, seemed to stop before my eyes, asking me to do something. I slipped into my

27

pants, walked down the hallway and into the living room. The house was asleep and dark. I could hear the big clock ticking like a heartbeat. I turned on the lamp. The big table was in disarray. Plates, coffee cups, and pieces of matzah lay scattered on the tablecloth. And one glass of wine. His wine!

I walked slowly to the glass, I moved close to it, my face very close, my eyes narrowing to the level of the liquid inside. How still everything was! I stared at the level: the wine seemed slightly lower in the glass. A faint ring, just above the liquid, went round the glass. That space between the ring and the liquid was Elijah's drink. Or had someone shaken the table, leaving the mark? No, it was Elijah. The proof in the glass. Believing is seeing!

Next thing—*bang*—I woke to a blazing light on the window. I had no recollection of getting back to my room. I dressed and hurried downstairs. The table had been cleared, the wineglass gone. Was it a dream, my coming down during the night? I couldn't remember, it was all becoming unreal in the sharp morning light. Without taking my breakfast I ran into the street. At that moment, Jimmy trotted by, his arms jackknifed against his chest like a long-distance runner, tongue lolling from his mouth.

I shouted to him, and he stopped. "Guess what, Jimmy? I had a dream. You'll never guess. It was an angel. Yeah, visiting our house. I swear."

"A lady angel?" he leered. "With clothes or naked?"

"It was Elijah," I said, my voice now low.

"Too bad!" He brayed like a jackass. "Maybe next time he'll bring his sister." We laughed and raced off to the beach together, the sun spreading into our bones, hoping for some excitement during the day.

The Author

NORMAN ROSTEN, poet, playwright, and novelist, is the author of six volumes of poetry, the latest entitled *Thrive Upon the Rock*. His plays, produced both on and off Broadway, have included *Mister Johnson* (based on the novel by Joyce Cary) and *Come Slowly, Eden*. His novels are *Under the Boardwalk* and *Over and Out*. A former Guggenheim Fellow, Mr. Rosten is the recipient of an award from the American Academy of Arts and Letters. *The Wineglass* is his first book for children.

The Illustrator

KAETHE ZEMACH is a working artist, illustrator, and computer operator and narrates a program on Station KPFA in Berkeley, California. She is the daughter of Margot and Harve Zemach.

This is her first book for children.